WELCOME TO
PASSPORT TO READING
A beginning reader's ticket to a brand-new world!

Every book in this program is designed to build read-along and read-alone skills, level by level, through engaging and enriching stories. As the reader turns each page, he or she will become more confident with new vocabulary, sight words, and comprehension.

These PASSPORT TO READING levels will help you choose the perfect book for every reader.

READING TOGETHER
Read short words in simple sentence structures together to begin a reader's journey.

READING OUT LOUD
Encourage developing readers to sound out words in more complex stories with simple vocabulary.

READING INDEPENDENTLY
Newly independent readers gain confidence reading more complex sentences with higher word counts.

READY TO READ MORE
Readers prepare for chapter books with fewer illustrations and longer paragraphs.

This book features sight words from the educator-supported Dolch Sight Words List. This encourages the reader to recognize commonly used vocabulary words, increasing reading speed and fluency.

For more information, please visit passporttoreadingbooks.com.

Enjoy the journey!

Little, Brown and Company

Hachette Book Group
1290 Avenue of the Americas, New York, NY 10104
Visit us at lb-kids.com

Little, Brown and Company is a division of Hachette Book Group, Inc.
The Little, Brown name and logo are trademarks of Hachette Book Group, Inc.

The publisher is not responsible for websites (or their content)
that are not owned by the publisher.

First Edition: July 2015
Meet Tinker Bell, Meet Vidia, Meet Zarina the Pirate Fairy, and *Meet Periwinkle*
originally published in 2014 by Little, Brown and Company.
Meet Fawn the Animal-Talent Fairy originally published in 2015
by Little, Brown and Company.

ISBN 978-0-316-33739-7 (paper over board) — ISBN 978-0-316-37855-0 (pbk)

10 9 8 7 6 5 4 3 2 1

SC

Printed in China

Passport to Reading titles are leveled by independent reviewers applying the standards developed by Irene Fountas and Gay Su Pinnell in *Matching Books to Readers: Using Leveled Books in Guided Reading*, Heinemann, 1999.

Meet the Fairies
A Collection of
Reading Adventures

LITTLE, BROWN AND COMPANY
New York • Boston

Table of Contents

Meet Tinker Bell

Adapted by Celeste Sisler

Illustrated by the Disney Storybook Art Team

LITTLE, BROWN AND COMPANY
New York • Boston

Attention, Disney Fairies fans!
Look for these words when you read
this story. Can you spot them all?

Silvermist

fireflies

owl

mouse

It is a big day for the fairies

who live in Pixie Hollow.

A new fairy is born.

Her name is Tinker Bell.

Queen Clarion tells Tinker Bell

she is born of laughter,

clothed in cheer,

and that happiness brought her here.

Each fairy has a talent.

What is Tinker Bell's talent?

The fairies give her light,

water, and flowers.

Nothing happens.

The fairies give Tinker Bell a hammer.

It glows.

Tinker Bell has found her talent!

She is a tinker fairy.

Tinkers fix things.

The other tinker fairies

welcome Tinker Bell.

Bobble and Clank show her
Pixie Hollow.

Then Tinker Bell meets Fairy Mary.

Fairy Mary is the head tinker.

"Being a tinker stinks,"
Tinker Bell tells Fairy Mary.
Tinker Bell wants to try
other talents.

Silvermist is a water fairy.

But Tink is not good with water.

She makes a splash.

Tink tries to be a light fairy.

The fireflies chase her away.

Tinker Bell tries to be an animal fairy.

She wants to help the baby owl.

But she scares the owl.

Tinker Bell keeps trying.

She tries to ride

Cheese the mouse.

Tinker Bell and Cheese
crash into the gate.
It opens.
All the Thistles run out.

The fairies are getting ready
for the spring season.
The Thistles run this way and that.
They run over the berries and seeds
for spring.

Tinker Bell made this mess.

Queen Clarion is upset.

How will they get ready

for spring now?

Tinker Bell has an idea.

She asks Bobble and Clank for help.

They make tools to make new things
for spring.

Tinker Bell saves spring
using her tinker talent.
All the fairies are happy.
The happiest fairy is
Queen Clarion.

Tinker Bell is happy.
She is a tinker fairy
and proud of it!

Meet Vidia

Adapted by Celeste Sisler

LITTLE, BROWN AND COMPANY
New York • Boston

Attention, Disney Fairies fans!
Look for these words when you read
this story. Can you spot them all?

butterfly

crickets

cage

cat

Tinker Bell and the fairies

fly to the Mainland

to get ready for summer.

One fairy paints lines and dots
on a butterfly.
Other fairies teach crickets
how to sing!

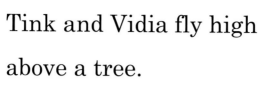

Tink and Vidia fly high
above a tree.
They see a car drive by
and follow it.

Two humans get out of the car.

Tink gets close to hear them.

"I wish it were summer all year long,"

says the girl.

"Yes, Lizzy," says her father.

They go inside the house.

Tink and Vidia fly around
to the backyard.
They see a fairy house.
Lizzy must have made it.
"Wow," says Tink.

Tinker Bell goes inside.

"This could be a trap!"
Vidia shouts.

"It is safe," says Tink.

Vidia slams the door

as a joke.

It sticks shut!

Tink is trapped inside!

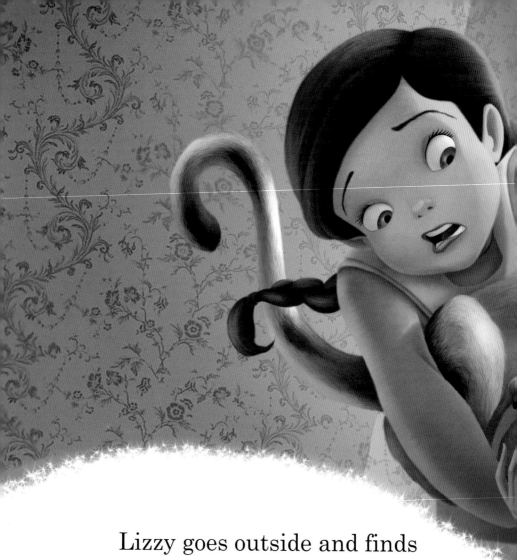

Lizzy goes outside and finds

Tink in the fairy house.

She brings her inside.

Vidia flies to a window.

She sees Tink in a cage.

She also sees a mean cat!

Vidia races back to the fairies.

She says Tinker Bell

needs their help.

Clank and Bobble

will make a boat.

Vidia leads the way,

and the fairies set sail.

They come to a waterfall.

The boat goes down!

They work together and

make it to the shore safely.

Vidia finds a road.

She takes a step and

gets stuck in the mud!

The fairies help pull her out.

Vidia is sad.

She feels bad for Tink.

"This is not your fault," says Rosetta.

They will save Tink together!

"Faith, trust, and pixie dust!"

they shout.

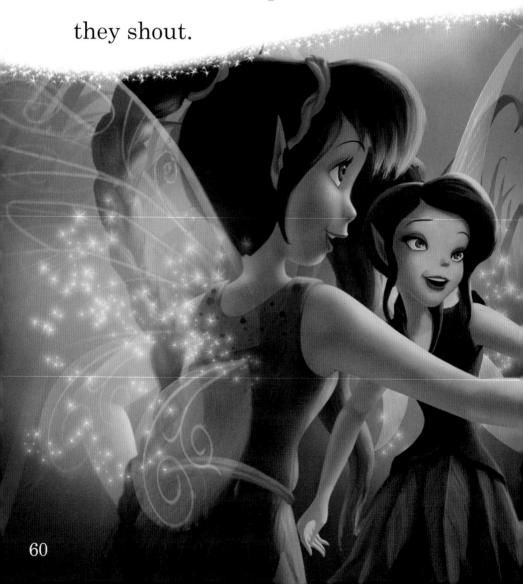

The fairies sneak into
Lizzy's house.
The cat jumps out!
The fairies run fast
and get away.

Vidia finds Tink in Lizzy's room.

She learns that Tink and Lizzy

are now friends!

Lizzy frees Tink.

The new friends
have a picnic.
Vidia is happy that
Tink is safe.
The fairies go home.

Meet Zarina
the Pirate Fairy

By Lucy Rosen

Illustrated by the Disney Storybook Art Team

LB

LITTLE, BROWN AND COMPANY

New York • Boston

Attention, Disney Fairies fans!
Look for these words when you read
this story. Can you spot them all?

Pixie Hollow

orange pixie dust

pirate

ship

Pixie Hollow is a magical place.
It is home to the
Never Land fairies.

The fairies have special talents.

Tinker Bell invents things.

She is a tinker fairy!

Iridessa is a light fairy.
She makes sunbeams
and rainbows!

Rosetta is a
garden fairy.
Plants bloom when
she is around.

Zarina is a dust-keeper fairy.

She helps tie up pixie dust.

Pixie dust can make things fly.

Zarina loves to learn
new things.
She asks a lot about
how pixie dust works.

It is Zarina's turn to help
work with Blue Pixie Dust.
She watches Fairy Gary
add the dust drop by drop.

Zarina dreams of creating
different colors of pixie dust.

At home, Zarina tries to make other kinds of pixie dust.

A tiny speck of
Blue Pixie Dust
falls out of her hair.

She adds it to a bowl
of regular pixie dust.

In a flash,

the dust turns orange!

"It worked!" she shouts.

Zarina invites Tinker Bell

to her house to see

the new pixie dust.

"You found orange pixie dust?"

asks Tinker Bell.

"No, Tink," says Zarina,

"I made orange pixie dust."

"That has never been done before,"
says Tinker Bell.

Zarina asks Tink to stir
another bowl.

They make purple pixie dust.
"Purple equals fast-flying
talent!" cries Zarina.
Tinker Bell is scared.

Zarina is excited.

She makes more and more

colors of dust.

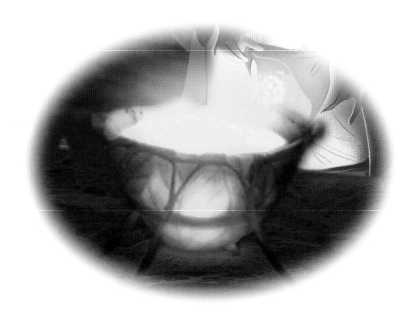

Zarina makes pink
garden-talent dust.
It spills onto a plant,
and vines grow out of
Zarina's house.

The vines grow
through Pixie Hollow.
They destroy the
Dust Depot!

Fairy Gary tells Zarina she
cannot be a dust-keeper fairy.
Zarina feels sad, so she flies
away from Pixie Hollow.

The fairies do not see
Zarina for a long time.
She comes back
to steal the Blue Pixie Dust!
The fairies chase her.

They find Zarina on a pirate ship.

She is wearing pirate clothes.

She has new pirate friends.

Something is not right!

The fairies follow
Zarina until she
is alone.
"Why are you
doing this?"
Tinker Bell asks.

Zarina explains that she will make pixie dust for the pirates. "This is exactly where I belong," Zarina says.

"Zarina, do not do this!"

Tinker Bell cries.

"Come back home."

"I am so sorry,"

Zarina says.

She hugs her friends.

The girls take control of the
pirate ship.
They take the ship and the Blue
Pixie Dust back to Pixie Hollow.

Meet Periwinkle

Adapted by Celeste Sisler

LITTLE, BROWN AND COMPANY
New York • Boston

Attention, Disney Fairies fans!
Look for these words when you read
this story. Can you spot them all?

owl

basket

book

snow

Tinker Bell and Fairy Mary
are making baskets.

Each owl takes one basket
to the Winter Woods.
Frost fairies use them
to collect snowflakes.

Warm fairies cannot go
to the Winter Woods.
The cold hurts their wings.
Tinker Bell is curious.

She looks on with Fawn as
the animals get ready to
cross into the Winter Woods.

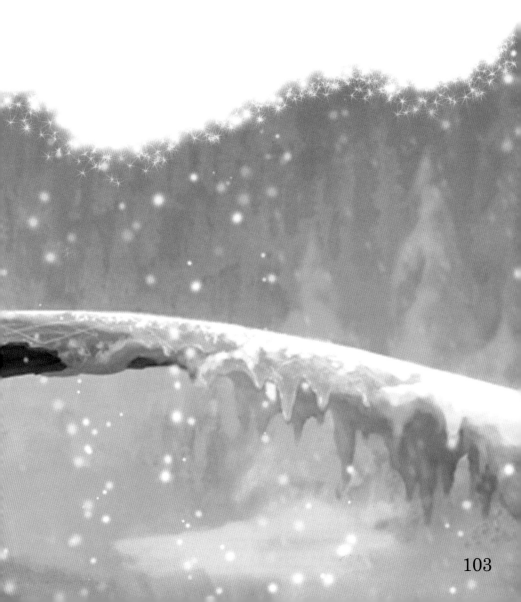

Tink wants to learn more.
She goes to the library
and takes out a book by
the Keeper.

The next day, Tink
goes to find the Keeper.
The Keeper is in
the Winter Woods.
She hides in a basket
and flies away.

Tink lands in the Winter Woods.

She hides behind the basket.

Her book falls out.

The ruler of the Winter Woods
sees it and gets mad.
"Return this book
to the Keeper," he tells a fairy.
Tink follows the fairy!

The fairy leads Tink
to the Hall of Winter.
The Keeper and
a frost fairy are there.
The frost fairy's name
is Periwinkle.

Their wings start to
sparkle and shine.
Tink and Peri fly
near each other.
The Keeper smiles.

The Keeper takes Tink and Peri
to a special room.

He shows them their past.

The two fairies were born
of the same laugh,
and then it split in two.
Tink and Peri are sisters!

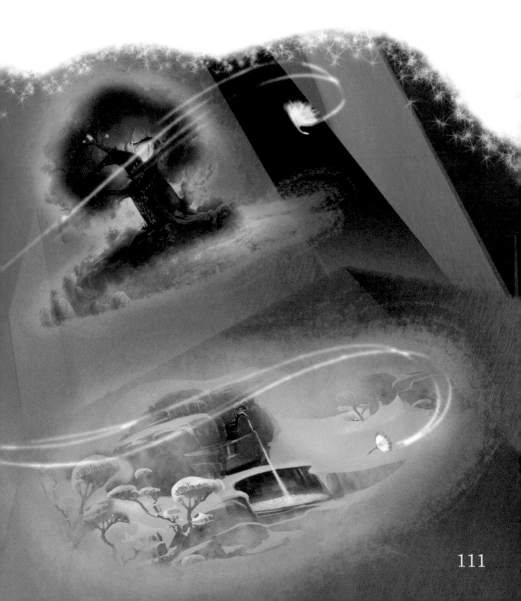

They are so happy!

Periwinkle takes Tink sledding.

She shows Tink her Found Things.

They build a fire
together, too.

Soon, Tink has to go home.
The sisters hug good-bye.

Peri wants to visit Pixie Hollow.

Tink and her friends

build a snow machine.

They hope it will help Peri stay cold.

Bobble and Clank help
Tinker Bell bring the
machine to the border
of Pixie Hollow.
Peri is there.

Periwinkle flies up
to the machine.
Snowflakes encircle
her wings.

The snow machine works.

Peri's wings are safe!

Periwinkle meets all of
Tink's friends and shows
them her frost talent.
It makes the fairies smile.

But soon it gets warmer.

Periwinkle's wings start to fall.

She needs to fly back to

the Winter Woods.

Suddenly, the snow machine
slides into a waterfall.
It gets stuck!

It turns on and
starts making snow.
Pixie Hollow begins
to freeze!

Tinker Bell asks Peri for
help from the frost fairies.
"Their frost can protect the tree,"
Tink explains to Fairy Mary
and the queen.

The frost fairies arrive and get to work right away.

The frost fairies freeze
the Pixie Dust Tree.
The sun comes out and
melts the frost.
The tree starts making
dust again!

Thanks to Periwinkle
and the frost fairies,
Pixie Hollow is saved!
Everyone is happy.

Meet Fawn

the Animal-Talent Fairy

By Jennifer Fox

Illustrated by the Disney Storybook Art Team

LITTLE, BROWN AND COMPANY

New York • Boston

Attention, Disney Fairies fans!
Look for these words when you read
this story. Can you spot them all?

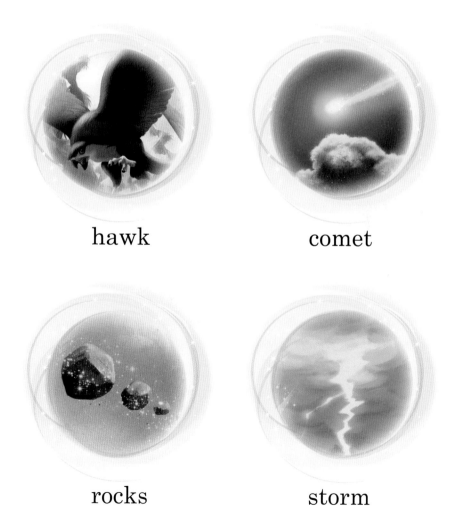

hawk

comet

rocks

storm

Fawn loves animals
with all her heart.

She wants to
help every critter
in the forest.

Fawn will even help out a baby hawk.

"Hawks eat fairies!"

Tink warns.

Fawn tells Tink that is not true.

Fawn fixes the hawk's wing.

"Hawk!" an animal fairy shouts.

Three new hawks fly in.

"Everyone, get inside," a fairy says.

Everyone is scared.

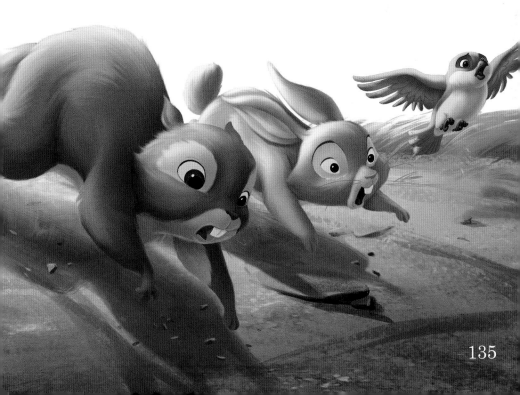

A scout fairy gets the
baby hawk under a net.

Queen Clarion says
Fawn should not bring
dangerous animals into
Pixie Hollow.

Fawn tries very hard

to follow this rule.

Yet when she hears a roar
in the forest, she follows
a trail of paw prints.

She finds a big and scary creature.

He is also fluffy.

"Hey, big guy," says Fawn.

"What are you?"

He is a NeverBeast.

The NeverBeast was
asleep for many years.
Then a comet woke him up.

Fawn decides to be his friend.

She names him Gruff and

helps him with his hurt paw.

Gruff builds towers of rocks.

Fawn adds a few.

"Now we are talking," she says.

Back home,
the scout fairies find
signs of the NeverBeast.
They find a trail and
bite marks.

They think a dangerous
animal is in Pixie Hollow!

The other fairies try to catch Gruff.

"Follow me,"
Fawn says to Gruff.
She knows in her
heart that he is good.
She will prove it
to the fairies.

A big storm comes.

It lights up the sky.

Fawn shows the others

how Gruff protects them.

He blocks the lightning.

Gruff's job is done.

He is tired,

but Pixie Hollow is safe.

The fairies walk him
back to his cave.

Gruff rests his head
on a pillow.
It is time for him
to go back to sleep.
"I love you, Gruff!"
says Fawn.

The big furry beast will
always hold a special
place in her heart.

THE END!

Read more

adventures!

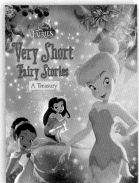

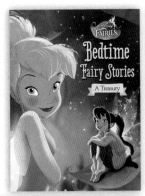

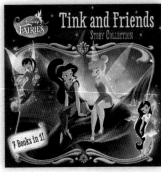

Don't miss these action-packed Disney FAIRIES TinkerBell AND THE LEGEND OF THE NEVERBEAST titles!

CHECKPOINTS IN THIS BOOK ✓

Meet Tinker Bell

WORD COUNT	GUIDED READING LEVEL	NUMBER OF DOLCH SIGHT WORDS
296	K	54

Meet Vidia

WORD COUNT	GUIDED READING LEVEL	NUMBER OF DOLCH SIGHT WORDS
310	J	62

Meet Zarina the Pirate Fairy

WORD COUNT	GUIDED READING LEVEL	NUMBER OF DOLCH SIGHT WORDS
418	L	63

Meet Periwinkle

WORD COUNT	GUIDED READING LEVEL	NUMBER OF DOLCH SIGHT WORDS
431	J	67

Meet Fawn the Animal-Talent Fairy

WORD COUNT	GUIDED READING LEVEL	NUMBER OF DOLCH SIGHT WORDS
306	J	70